Skateboard Cops

By Dot Meharry

Illustrated by James Hart

Pearson Australia
(a division of Pearson Australia Group Pty Ltd)
707 Collins Street, Melbourne, Victoria 3008
PO Box 23360, Melbourne, Victoria 8012
www.pearson.com.au

First published 2010 by Pearson Australia
2017 2016 2015
10 9 8 7 6 5 4 3 2

Publisher: Simone Calderwood
Illustrator: James Hart
Editor: Fiona Cooke
Designer: Glen McClay
Copyright & Pictures Editor: Helen Mammides
Project Editor: Aisling Coughlan
Production Controller: Claire Henry
Printed and bound in Australia by Pegasus Media & Logistics

ISBN 978 1 4425 2813 0

Pearson Australia Group Pty Ltd ABN 40 004 245 943

Contents

A Glossary of Skateboard Words

grind to slide along an edge using the skateboard wheel trucks (or axles)

handplant when the skateboarder balances on one hand at the top of the ramp

kickflip a move in which the skateboarder jumps and spins the board into a barrel roll with their foot before landing on it

ollie a skateboard jump, where the board travels with the skateboarder

powerslide a sharp turn that skateboarders use to come to a quick stop

ramp a high-walled, curved surface built especially for skateboarding

slide the same as a grind, but using the skateboard deck (board)

Chapter 1

Waiting for Frankie

ZAK GRABBED his new skateboard and safety gear from the back seat.

"See ya later, Mum," he said, getting out of the car. He felt nervous. It was his first time at the skate park. Usually he rode his board at his cousin's house. Frankie had her own ramp. She even had a rail to slide along.

Zak looked up and down for Frankie. There was no sign of her. She'd told him she would be there early.

While he waited, he watched some boys use the ramp. Their moves were snappy and smooth, just like they were supposed to be. They did ollies and kickflips, spinning their boards in the air. Some did grinds on the edges and slides on the rails. They all knew how to get off when a trick went wrong, and land safely.

One of the boys walked over to Zak. Zak noticed he didn't have a board.

"Hey," the boy said. "I haven't seen you here before. First time, is it?"

Zak nodded.

The boy took Zak's new skateboard from him and looked at it.

"Nice," he said, rubbing his hand over the deck. He turned the board over. He looked at the shiny trucks and clean wheels. "You wanna have a go?" he asked.

Zak nodded again. The boy shouted at the skateboarders on the ramp and waved them off. Flicking their boards up into their hands, they did as he asked.

"New guy," he said, pointing his thumb at Zak. "He wants a turn."

"Cool, Jake," they answered.

The boys joked among themselves as they waited for Zak to put on his safety gear.

Where was Frankie? Zak wondered again. *He should have waited until she got there.*

"Go!" said Jake, as Zak pushed off. The others joined in.

"Go on! Yeah! Go on!"

Zak kept a look out for Frankie as he did some moves. It made him lose concentration and make mistakes. He couldn't even do an ollie properly.

"Bend your knees," shouted one of the boys.

Zak's first time at the skate park wasn't going so well. He was bailing out of doing simple moves that were usually easy for him. He felt silly.

Rolling to a stop, he picked up his board.

"Thanks," he said to the boys watching.

Chapter 2

Trouble

AS ZAK LEFT THE RAMP, Jake stood where he was, waiting for him. He reached for the new skateboard.

"My turn," he said.

Zak hugged his board to his chest. He didn't like the way Jake was standing over him. He tried to speak, but his words were lost somewhere in his head.

"What d'ya reckon? It's my turn, isn't it?" said Jake, looking around at the other boys.

The boys didn't answer. They looked down at the ground in front of them as if they hadn't heard. Jake said it again.

"It's my turn, isn't it!"

One of the boys lifted his head. He'd been on the ramp when Zak first arrived at the skate park.

"The board belongs to him," he said quietly. "Leave him alone."

Jake glared at the boy who had spoken up. Zak's heart beat faster and faster. It beat so loudly, he was sure Jake could hear it.

Suddenly, Jake snatched Zak's board out of his arms and held it above his head. "Look, Matt. The kid's going to let me have a turn!" he shouted to the boy who had spoken up.

The boy called Matt dropped his head and stared at the ground. He didn't answer Jake.

Zak watched as Jake tucked his new skateboard under his arm.

"You can have your board back tomorrow," Jake said. He headed towards the tunnel that went under the railway line next to the skate park. All the boys except Matt followed him.

Zak's eyes filled with tears as they walked away. He looked around again for Frankie. Where was she?

It had taken Frankie longer to change the wheels on her board than she'd thought. She hoped Zak was all right.

As she rode down the footpath, she pressed down on the back of her board, lifting and twisting the nose to change direction. At last, the skate park was in sight. She put a foot down and gave herself a push.

There was no-one on the ramp when Frankie got there. She looked around for Zak but couldn't see him anywhere. Suddenly, she heard her name. "*Frankieeeeee!* Over here!"

Zak was at the car park and someone was with him. She picked up her board and walked over to them.

"Why aren't you at the ramp?" she asked. "You've got your safety gear on."

"I'm waiting for Mum," Zak answered.

He told her about Jake.

"And this is Matt," he said. "He stayed with me when Jake and the other boys went away."

Matt was sitting on the deck of his skateboard. His arms were wrapped around his knees. He looked miserable.

"I'm sorry," he said. "Jake scares me."

Frankie knew which boy he meant. There'd been trouble at the skate park ever since Jake had come to live in the city. She swung her backpack to the ground. The deck of a skateboard poked out of the top.

"I brought this for you to use, Zak," she said, pulling it out. "I didn't know you'd got your new one."

"It was supposed to be a surprise," said Zak sadly.

"Well, let's try to find Jake and see if we can get your new board back," she said. She stepped onto her own board.

"What are you waiting for? Let's go!"

Chapter 3

A Surprise for Jake

FRANKIE RODE towards the tunnel where Jake and the other boys had gone. She looked back at Zak and Matt. They were right behind her.

Watching for pedestrians, they freewheeled down the path into the tunnel and under the railway line. Then the three of them stepped off their boards and carried them up the rise, onto the walkway on the other side.

There were crowds of people jogging or walking down the walkway. Frankie looked up and down, wondering which way Jake and the others had gone. They could be anywhere.

Suddenly, she pointed to her right. "There!" she cried.

In the distance, skateboarders were spread out along the walkway. They would have to hurry.

The three boards made a racket on the concrete walkway. The sight of Zak, Frankie and Matt coming towards them was enough to make most people step out of their way. The people yelled at them to slow down.

Zak knew they were right, but he wanted his skateboard back.

Close to a corner, Frankie signalled the two boys to stop. She was already looking around the corner to see where Jake and the other boys were. Then she pointed again and looked back.

"It's him," she whispered. "He's alone."

Zak and Matt poked their heads around Frankie so they could see, too. Jake was sitting on a wooden seat not far away. He was rolling Zak's skateboard up and down with his foot. His head hung down as if he was watching it go backwards and forwards underneath him. The other boys were nowhere to be seen.

"Wait here," whispered Frankie.

She stepped onto her board and pushed herself around the corner. Jake lifted his head as Frankie did a wheelie stop in front of him. He knew her face. He'd seen her at the skate park a few times. She was a good skater.

"Hi, Jake," she said. "What are you doing here?"

“Nothing,” he grunted.

“That’s a cool board,” Frankie went on, pointing to the board under his foot. “Where’d you get it?”

“My dad!” answered Jake.

“D’ya mind if I have a look?” she asked.

Jake stood up. He did mind, and he didn’t feel like talking about the skateboard. He got ready to ride off down the walkway again.

Frankie put a foot in front of the wheels.

"That board isn't yours," she said. "You took it off my cousin at the skate park. He wants it back."

Jake stared at her. She was that guy's cousin? How did she find him?

Chapter 4

I Want My Skateboard Back!

FRANKIE WAS TAKEN by surprise when Jake shoved her. She staggered backwards and tumbled heavily onto the walkway.

Jake grabbed her board and sent it rolling down the walkway. Then, without a word, he pushed off on Zak's board and headed back the way he had come.

Zak and Matt saw Jake shove Frankie over and roll her skateboard away from her. They saw him coming towards them.

"Oh no!" gasped Matt. "He's coming this way!"

Zak's heart beat louder and louder.

"What are we going to do?" he cried.

There was nowhere to hide. Jake would see them when he came round the corner. The two boys stared at each other. They wouldn't be able to stop Jake. Frankie couldn't.

They could hear the wheels of the skateboard coming closer and closer. As Jake carved round the corner, Zak's eyes locked onto the skateboard under his feet. He'd chosen it carefully. The wheels were fast and smooth. The deck was a good size. He'd even put extra grip tape on the deck so his feet wouldn't slip off when he did tricks.

Suddenly, Zak felt angry that Jake had made them feel scared.

"We'll stop him," he said to Matt.

Zak had let Jake take his board off him once. He wasn't about to let him get away with it a second time.

Zak leapt out and grabbed hold of Jake's T-shirt as he cruised past.

"Hey! What the—" cried Jake, wobbling dangerously. "Let me go!"

But Zak didn't let go. Jake turned his head to see who was holding onto him.

"I want my skateboard back!" yelled Zak.

Jake pushed the tail of the skateboard downwards so it dragged along the walkway, and stopped.

"Come and get it then," he said. He placed one foot on either side of the skateboard and waited for Zak to let go of his T-shirt.

But Zak didn't let go. Still holding on, he slid feet-first towards the tail of the skateboard between Jake's legs. He kicked it as hard as he could.

The skateboard shot away like a bullet and zoomed down the walkway.

"Get the board, Matt!" Zak shouted, letting the T-shirt go. He dropped to the ground, wrapped his arms around one of Jake's legs, and held on tight.

Chapter 5

Skateboard Cops

DROPPING HIS OWN BOARD to the ground, Matt took a deep breath before pushing off. Passing Jake and Zak, he headed after Zak's runaway board. Faster and faster, he sped down the walkway until he caught up with it.

Matt reached down and caught the board by the tail. Only then did he dare look back. Zak was struggling to hold onto Jake. Jake was a lot bigger and stronger than the other boy.

Suddenly, there was a shout from behind.

Frankie was speeding towards Jake and Zak on her board. Stamping down with her back foot, she snapped the board back and jumped into the air. The board lifted with her. She tucked her legs up to her chest and grabbed the nose of the flying board.

Jake and Zak dived onto the walkway as Frankie sailed over them. She let go of the board and came down on the other side. Then she did a wheelie stop and headed back to the boys, who were spread-eagled on the walkway.

Jake lay still. He couldn't believe what had just happened to him. He had just been taken down with the best ollie he'd ever seen.

Matt joined the joggers and walkers who were gathering around Frankie and Zak.

"Can I call the police for you?" asked a woman.

"Yes, please," said Frankie. "Ask for Constable Moore. He's my dad."

Jake groaned. The girl's father was a policeman!

When Frankie's dad arrived, Zak and Frankie told him what had happened.

"You have some explaining to do, young man," said Frankie's dad. He reached down to help Jake up.

Frankie's dad turned to Frankie and the two boys.

"You did well," he said. "You were good cops."

"Skateboard cops," said Frankie with a grin.

Chapter 6

Changes

THE NEXT SATURDAY, Frankie's dad joined Jake, Frankie, Zak and Matt at the skate park. He called the skateboarders together.

"The skate park needs to be a safe place for everyone who comes here. It will be closed if you don't make changes," he said. "It's up to you to look after each other."

The boys who had followed Jake looked embarrassed. They knew they should have looked out for Zak last weekend.

"Jake has something to say to you," Frankie's dad went on.

Jake looked at the ground.

"I'm sorry for the trouble I've caused," he said quietly, looking up.

"Well, Zak got his board back," said Frankie, "and that was the best ollie I've ever done!"

"And we got to be skateboard cops," added Zak. "Frankie's dad is getting T-shirts made for us."

"I'd like to be a skateboard cop," said a boy.

"Me too," said another.

Frankie's dad held up his hands. "I'm happy to get T-shirts made for all of you. But you have to earn a skateboard cop's T-shirt. Make the skate park a safe place by looking out for each other. As for Jake, I know he's sorry for what he did, but he is still banned for a month."

Jake nodded.

"By the way," Frankie's dad went on. "There's going to be a competition in about six weeks' time. Practise your moves. I'll try to get a big name like Deano to come and give a demo."

Everyone looked puzzled.

"Deano?" they asked. "Who's he?"

Frankie laughed. "He's a really good skateboarder. You wait and see."

After Frankie's dad drove Jake home, everyone sat on the ramp and talked about what had happened.

"Jake's dad was killed in a tractor accident," explained Frankie. "His mum brought the family to the city so she could find work. Jake misses his dad and the farm. What happened makes him feel angry."

Everyone was sorry that Jake had lost his dad.

"My dad's going to help him," said Frankie.

Chapter 7

Competition Day

SIX WEEKS LATER, people gathered at the skate park for the competition. Whole families had come to watch. It had been advertised in the newspaper. Prizes had been donated by shops in the city.

When Frankie's dad turned on the microphone, the crowd went quiet.

"Welcome, everyone," he said. "It's good to see so many of you here. As you know, the kids have a great skate park. In this competition, they are going to show you what they can do."

All morning, skateboarders showed off the tricks they had been practising. Then, while the judges were deciding on the winner, Frankie introduced the next skateboarder.

"And now we have… the incredible Deano!"

Everyone waited. Suddenly, a man ran out and onto the ramp with his board. The crowd clapped and cheered every time he did a trick. They gasped when he did a handplant, balancing his whole weight on one hand, and then a spectacular kickflip.

Deano was good. When he finished on a powerslide and lifted his board into the air, the crowd chanted, "Deano! Deano!"

"You were great, Constable Moore," cried the skateboarders when the demonstration was over.

"I was skateboarding before you kids were born," he laughed.

He winked at Jake. Jake smiled. He'd worked at the skate park all day. He'd helped kids with their safety gear. He'd helped give out drinks and food. He liked being with Frankie's dad.

That afternoon, Zak and Matt went back to Frankie's house. They cleaned their boards and checked the trucks and wheels.

Suddenly Frankie stopped. "I've been thinking," she said. "Jake doesn't have a skateboard of his own. He could have my old skateboard. You don't need it any more, Zak."

"We could do it up for him," exclaimed Zak excitedly. "You know—clean the bearings and sand down the rough edges on the deck."

"And make it look really cool with stickers," added Matt.

Frankie looked at the two boys.

"Well—what are we waiting for!"